W9-BEG-193

Noise in the Night

Written by
Bruce Witty

Illustrated by
Miriam Nerlove

Colored by
Gail L. Suess

Late at night, as I lay in bed,
I heard a noise go through my head.

I heard a scratch and then a squeak.
I heard a thump and then a creak.
I heard a noise below my bed.
Then over by the wall it spread.

Up the wall into the ceiling,
I thought I heard
something squealing.

I rose to see what it could be.
I took a light so I could see.

I opened up the attic door
and heard a creaking on the floor.
"Who is there?" I whispered low.
"Who is there?" I want to know.

"I am your house,"
a deep voice said.
"Why aren't you asleep in bed?"

"Well, you woke me up
with all your noise.
You almost woke up
all my toys!"

"I'm sorry," my house said to me. "But I have to stretch and yawn, you see."

"I have to stretch and move a bit,
because all day long I just sit."

"So at night, while you're asleep,
I wiggle around and stretch my feet."

"I squeak and groan
and moan and creak,
I stretch myself up to my peak."

"Oh," I said. "Yes, I see.
You have to stretch, I do agree.
But now I must go back to sleep.
So please be still without a peep."

The next thing I remember,
I was sitting up in bed.
I thought about the night before
and what my house had said.

Was it all a dream,
now that night had turned to day?
Or when I go back to bed,
will my house have more to say?

The End